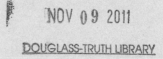

Little, Brown and Company

Hachette Book Group
237 Park Avenue, New York, NY 10017
Visit our website at www.lb-kids.com

Little, Brown and Company is a division of Hachette Book Group, Inc.
The Little, Brown name and logo are trademarks of
Hachette Book Group, Inc.

The publisher is not responsible for websites (or their content) that are not owned by
the publisher.

First Edition: October 2011

The characters and events portrayed in this book are fictitious.
Any similarity to real persons, living or dead, is coincidental
and not intended by the author.

ISBN: 978-0-316-18311-6

10 9 8 7 6 5 4 3 2 1

WOR

Printed in the United States of America

FROGS ARE FUNNY!

THE MOST SENSATIONAL, INSPIRATIONAL, CELEBRATIONAL, MUPPETATIONAL MUPPETS JOKE BOOK EVER!

BY **The Muppets**   WITH **Brandon T. Snider**

Little, Brown and Company
New York   Boston

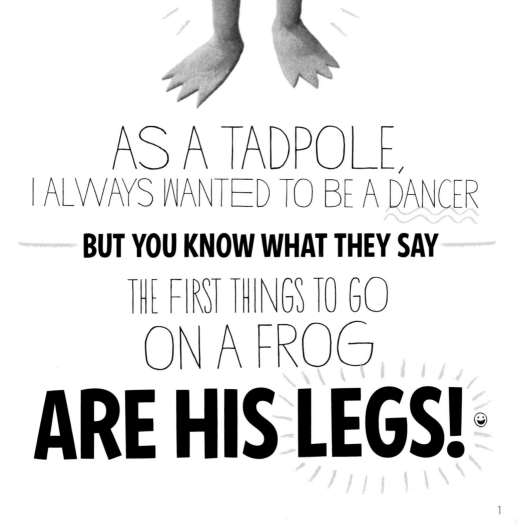

AS A TADPOLE,
I ALWAYS WANTED TO BE A DANCER

BUT YOU KNOW WHAT THEY SAY

THE FIRST THINGS TO GO
ON A FROG
ARE HIS LEGS! ☺

I'M SO NERVOUS!

IF I'M NOT **FUNNY,** I WON'T KNOW HOW TO LIVE WITH MYSELF.

THEN YOU'LL HAVE TO GET A **NEW APARTMENT, WON'T YOU?** ☺

HA HA HA HA HA HA HA

MY DEAR
GONZO,
I KNOW IT WILL BE
PAINFUL FOR A WHILE,
BUT IN TIME YOU SHALL
FORGET ALL ABOUT ME.

But I already have.

OH.

YES, I FOUND SOMEBODY ELSE.

OH, UH, WELL . . . UH, YEAH, WHAT, UH—
WHAT'S SHE LIKE?

WELL, SHE'S NOTHING LIKE YOU AT ALL.
SHE'S BEEYOOO-TIFUL!

(CONT.)

SHE'S GOT THIS CUTE LITTLE NOSE,
AND SHE'S INTELLIGENT AND TALENTED,
AND I'M VERY HAPPY.

**You see, breaking up with you
isn't painful at all.**

NOT UNTIL NOW.

HI-YAH! ☺

I HAVE A DRESSING ROOM SO SMALL...

ALL THE MICE ARE HUNCHBACKS! ☺

HOW WOULD YOU LIKE A PORK CHOP?

HIII-YAH!

I'D LOVE TO BE ON BROADWAY.

Yeah, I can see your name in lights: **25 watts!**

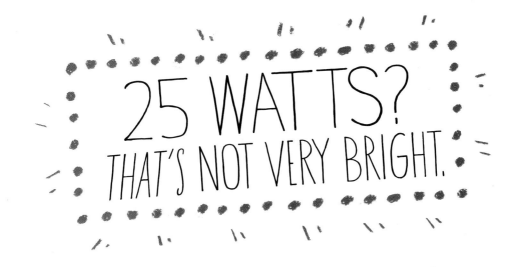

25 WATTS?
THAT'S NOT VERY BRIGHT.

Look who's talking! ☺

OH, NO, ANOTHER CHICKEN!

IF THEY KEEP BRINGING IN CHICKENS WE'RE GOING TO BE HERE TWENTY-FOUR HOURS.

WHAT DO YOU MEAN?

WE'LL HAVE TO WORK AROUND THE **CLUCK!** ☺

THAT GONZO IS **SO DUMB** THAT HE JUST HEARD WE'RE RUNNING SHORT ON WATER...

SO HE WANTS US TO DILUTE IT!

THIS IS THE MOST CONSISTENT SHOW I'VE EVER SEEN.

YES, IT GETS WORSE EVERY SINGLE WEEK! ☺

WELL, HOW LONG WILL IT TAKE TO FIX IT?

WE CAN'T! IT'S REALLY *LOST*! IT FELL OFF!

17

I JUST WANT TO KNOW MORE ABOUT THIS WEDDING SKETCH. I MEAN, I'VE GOT TO **learn my lines, Piggy.**

WELL, YOU ONLY HAVE ONE LINE.

I do?

EXACTLY. ☺

WELCOME AGAIN TO
Muppet Labs,
where the future is being made today.
AND HERE IT IS, FOLKS, THE PRODUCT YOU'VE ALL BEEN WAITING FOR:

THE NEW SOLID-STATE

GORILLA DETECTOR.

Yes, friends,

HOW MANY TIMES HAVE YOU AWAKENED AT NIGHT IN THE DARK AND SAID TO YOURSELF,

"Is there a gorilla in here?"

AND HOW MANY PEOPLE DO YOU KNOW WHOSE VACATIONS WERE RUINED BECAUSE

THEY WERE EATEN BY UNDETECTED GORILLAS? ☺

I HOPE YOU APPRECIATE THAT I'M DOING ALL **MY OWN STUNTS.** ☺

YOU SHOULD NEVER EAT THE COMEDIAN!

THEY TASTE FUNNY! HAAAAAA!

HA HA HA HA HA HA

HA HA HA HA HA HA HA HA HA HA

IN OUR HOUSE
WE USE PAPER PLATES.

Every night after dinner my wife ERASES the dishes. ☺

24

THIS SHOW IS GOOD FOR WHAT AILS ME.

WHAT AILS YOU?

INSOMNIA. ☺

I SHOULD KNOW BETTER THAN TO ASK A **CHICKEN.** ☺

HERE'S YOUR NEXT PATIENT.

Hey, this is just a shoe!

WHAT HAPPENED TO THE REST OF HIM?

Maybe he got cold feet! ☺

GUY WALKS
INTO A DINER.

THERE'S A HORSE BEHIND
THE COUNTER. THE GUY JUST
LOOKS AT THE HORSE AND SAYS,

"What's the matter?
Surprised to see me here?"

AND THE GUY SAYS,

"Yeah, did the cow
sell the place?" ☺

THIS APPLE HAS A WORM IN IT.

THAT'S NOT A WORM— IT'S MY TAIL! ☺

OH KERMIE, YOU WERE SO COURAGEOUS, **SO MAGNIFICENT!**

GEE, I DON'T KNOW WHAT TO SAY.

Say the *bear* was magnificent! After all, I did the driving!

AND I TOOK A HUNDRED-FOOT BELLY FLOP ONTO A MOVING CAR!

(CONT.)

35

WELL,
I DIDN'T THINK I'D LIVE TO SEE IT,
BUT FOR ONCE THEY'VE GIVEN US
SOMETHING OTHER THAN **SECOND-RATE**
ENTERTAINMENT!

WHAT'S
THAT?

THIRD-RATE ENTERTAINMENT!

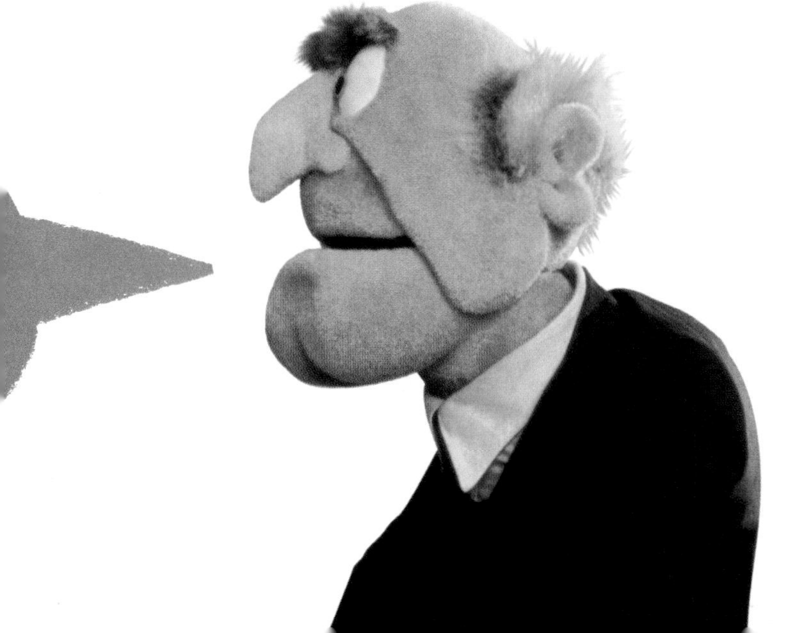

I'M LEARNING SPANISH FOR MY NEW ACT!

Oh, okay.

YEAH, YOU HAVE TO LEARN SPANISH IF YOU'RE GOING TO TRAIN MEXICAN

JUMPING

BEANS! ☺

YOU'RE SUCH A SMOOTH DANCER.
EVER SINCE WE'VE STARTED, I FEEL LIKE
MY FEET HAVE NEVER TOUCHED THE FLOOR.

They haven't.
You've been standing on mine. ☺

I GO WITH A LOVELY GIRL.
She's so bowlegged,
WHEN SHE STANDS
AROUND THE HOUSE,
SHE STANDS
AROUND THE HOUSE! ☺

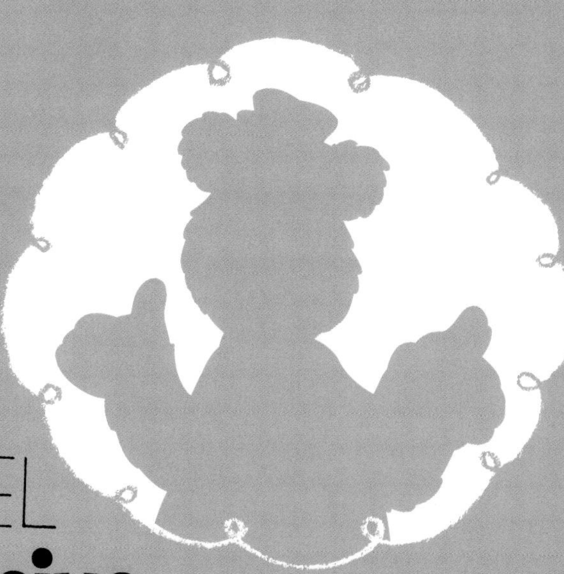

I STAYED
AT A HOTEL
so exclusive
THAT ROOM SERVICE WAS
AN UNLISTED NUMBER! ☺

**IRRI-TATED!
IRRI-TATED!**

DON'T WORRY, ANIMAL, YOUR BIG SCENE IS COMING UP.

YEAH, JUST BE COOL
AND EAT ANOTHER
SEAT CUSHION.

SEEEAT
CUSH-ION! ☺

I throw fish into the air, and then they sail away and come back to me!

I DON'T CARE ABOUT BOOMERANG FISH ACTS!

(CONT.)

YOU WILL ...

THEY'RE COMING BACK! ☺

AHEM. I WOULD JUST LIKE TO SAY A FEW WORDS ABOUT **NUDITY** IN THE WORLD TODAY. I, FOR ONE, AM JUST APPALLED BY IT.

WHY, DID YOU KNOW THAT UNDERNEATH THEIR CLOTHING, THE ENTIRE POPULATION OF THE WORLD IS WALKING AROUND COMPLETELY **NAKED?** HMM? IS THAT DISGUSTING?

AND IT'S NOT JUST PEOPLE, ALTHOUGH, GOODNESS KNOWS, THAT'S BAD ENOUGH. EVEN CUTE LITTLE DOGGIES AND PUSSYCATS CAN'T BE TRUSTED. UNDERNEATH THEIR FUR, AB-SO-LUTE-LY **NAKED!** AND IT'S NOT JUST THE QUADRIPEDS, EITHER. BIRDS, TOO! YES! BENEATH THOSE FINE FEATHERS, BIRDS WEAR **NOTHING! NOTHING AT ALL!**

ABSO- ...☺

THESE TWO CANNIBALS WERE TALKING.
ONE CANNIBAL SAYS TO THE OTHER CANNIBAL,

"WHO WAS THAT LADY
I SAW YOU WITH
LAST NIGHT?"

THE OTHER CANNIBAL SAYS,

"THAT WAS NO LADY– THAT WAS MY LUNCH!" ☺

I'LL SAY THIS FOR THEM, THEY DON'T SHOW FAVORITISM.

THEY OFFEND EVERYBODY! ☺

ANIMAL, WILL YOU STOP BUGGING ME?

GO DO SOMETHING TO CALM DOWN. GO FIND A HOBBY OR SOMETHING!

(CONT.)

I SUGGEST WE JUMP.

Are you crazy? THAT'S AT LEAST A HUNDRED FEET!

I DIDN'T SAY
IT WAS A GOOD
SUGGESTION. ☺

MAKE READY FOR THE CAPTAIN! LOLLYGAGGERS WILL SUFFER HIS WRATH!

Is the captain bad tempered?

IS HE BAD TEMPERED?
THE MAN IS A RAGING VOLCANO,
TORMENTED BY INNER DEMONS
THE LIKES OF WHICH MERE
MORTALS CANNOT FATHOM.

He's got <u>demons?</u>
Cool! ☺

MY HOUSE IS SO DIRTY...

MY DOG BURIES HIS BONES IN THE LIVING ROOM CARPET. ☺

WE GOT OUR **MONEY'S** WORTH TONIGHT!

BUT WE PAID NOTHING.

THAT'S WHAT WE GOT! ☺

WE WERE
IN JAIL FOR
FOUR HOURS,
GONZO.

GEE,
IT FELT LIKE
FORTY YEARS!

THIS IS GREAT, GONZO—
YOU POPPED THE FLASH
JUST BEFORE THE SOUP
LANDED ON HIS TIE.

YEAH, WELL, PHOTOGRAPHY IS AN ART. YOU'VE GOT TO HAVE THE RIGHT FILM, THE RIGHT EXPOSURE… AND YOU'VE GOT TO **SCREAM** JUST BEFORE THEY GET THE FOOD TO THEIR MOUTH. ☺

WE'RE GONNA CATCH THOSE THIEVES RED-HANDED!

WHAT COLOR ARE THEIR HANDS NOW? ☺

DR. BOB, CHICKENS DO NOT QUACK.

THEY DO WHEN THEY'RE YOUNG.

THEY DO?

Sure. If you drop an egg, it'll QUACK! ☺

DR. BUNSEN HONEYDEW HERE,
AT MUPPET LABS, WHERE THE
FUTURE IS BEING MADE TODAY.

NOW THE HONOR OF TASTING THIS FIRST
BATCH OF DELICIOUS PAPER CLIPS
GOES OF COURSE TO
MY HELPFUL AND
EAGER ASSISTANT,
BEAKER.

NUH UH!

NOW, BEAKER, WHAT IS THE MATTER?

MEE MEE MEE!

(CONT.)

OH, THAT'S VERY NAUGHTY, BEAKER!
NOW, YOU EAT THOSE CLIPS THIS MINUTE!
GO ON, EAT, THEY'RE NOT SO BAD. . . .
GO AHEAD.

**Mmmmmmm.
Mmm, mmm.
MEEP!!**

YES, FRIENDS, MUPPETS' EDIBLE PAPER CLIPS ARE DELICIOUS, NUTRITIOUS, AND NICKEL-PLATED. THEY'RE HANDY AROUND THE OFFICE, AND THEY ARE WONDERFUL AS A TV SNACK! FURTHERMORE, THEY ARE ABSOLUTELY HARMLESS—

Mee mee mee mee MEEEEEEEEE!!

...OR NEARLY SO. ☺

Same as always—
TERRIBLE! ☺

MY DEAR,
YOU ARE SO **BEAUTIFUL.**
HAVE I SEEN YOU IN THE MOVIES?

I DON'T THINK SO.
I hardly ever go!☺

Kermit, what are the cows here for?

WELL, THEY'RE HERE FOR RAY AND DALE'S CLOSING NUMBER.

What are they singing?

"Catch a Falling *Steer*"?
OR
"If *Heifer* Should I Leave You"?
WHAT ABOUT
"*Mooooooo* River"? ☺

HEY GUYS! LOOK AT THESE OLD PHOTOS I FOUND.

CAN YOU BELIEVE THAT '80S HAIRCUT I USED TO HAVE?

I LOOKED TOTALLY RIDICULOUS! ☺

NO, NAPPLES. ~~NAPPLES.~~ YOU PUT THEM ON PIES.

PIE-NAPPLES! ☺

TEN OR ELEVEN MILES AWAY!

YEAH, THAT'S THE
ROAD MANAGER.

HE'S THE MAN WITH
THE CONTACTS?

No, he's the man with the van. ☺

HAVE YOU HEARD
THE ONE ABOUT THIS
VERY **FAT** PIG?

HAVE YOU HEARD
THE ONE ABOUT THIS
VERY **FLAT** BEAR?

HIII-
YAH! ☺

A tap-dancing chicken act?

GONZO, I'VE NEVER HEARD OF ANYTHING AS RIDICULOUS AS A DANCING CHICKEN.

HOW ABOUT A
**TALKING
FROG?** ☺

I FIND THAT MOST PEOPLE DON'T <u>BELIEVE</u> WHAT OTHER PEOPLE TELL THEM.

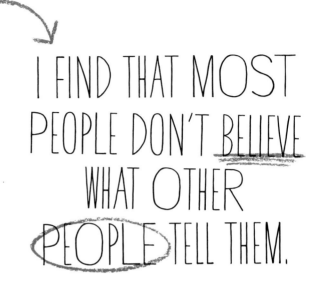

I don't think that's true. ☺

Will you love me forever?

I DON'T KNOW, BABY. ASK ME AGAIN IN A MILLION YEARS. ☺

KERMIT, PLEASE LET ME BE IN **Pigs in Space!**

YOU CAN'T.

(CONT.)

WHY CAN'T I BE IN **Pigs in Space?**

BECAUSE YOU'RE NOT A **PIG!**

Nobody's perfect. ☺

That does it! I am leaving!

WELL, DON'T YOU HAVE ANYTHING TO SAY TO ME BEFORE I GO?

I FINALLY FOUND THE
SURE WAY TO LOSE WEIGHT:

I bought a scale that lies! ☺

Oh, my heart!

It's going pitter, patter . . . pitter, patter.

YEAH, WELL,
MAYBE YOU'VE HAD
TOO MUCH COFFEE. ☺

I HEARD THAT THE PRESIDENT SAID YOU SHOULDN'T PANIC IF YOU DON'T HAVE A JOB.

That's easy for him to say—
HE'S GOT A JOB! ☺

TWO AMOEBAS WALKED OUT OF A BAR.

ONE AMOEBA SAYS TO THE OTHER,

"Say, is that the sun or the moon?"

THE OTHER AMOEBA SAYS,

"I don't know. I don't live around here."

HA HA HA HA HA HA HA

I don't know.
I don't live around here,
EITHER! ☺

TONIGHT I'M GOING TO PUT SOMETHING NEW IN MY ACT!

I WAS GOING TO GIVE BEAKER THE HONOR OF DEMONSTRATING THIS NEW DIESEL SHAVER.

That's a close shave
for Beaker either way. ☺

HEY, RIZZO, RELAX!
DON'T BE SO AFRAID.

I'VE GONE WAY BEYOND AFRAID. RIGHT NOW I'M SOMEWHERE BETWEEN **BED-WETTING** AND A **NEAR-DEATH EXPERIENCE.** ☺

Kissy-kissy?

UH, MISS PIGGY, WHILE I AM FLATTERED AT THIS DISPLAY OF AFFECTION, ALLOW ME TO REMIND YOU ONCE AGAIN THAT

I do not want you.

Oh, good, then can I have her?

(CONT.)

THAT IS KNOWN
AS GETTING
**TWO
TURKEYS**
WITH
**ONE
CHOP.** ☻

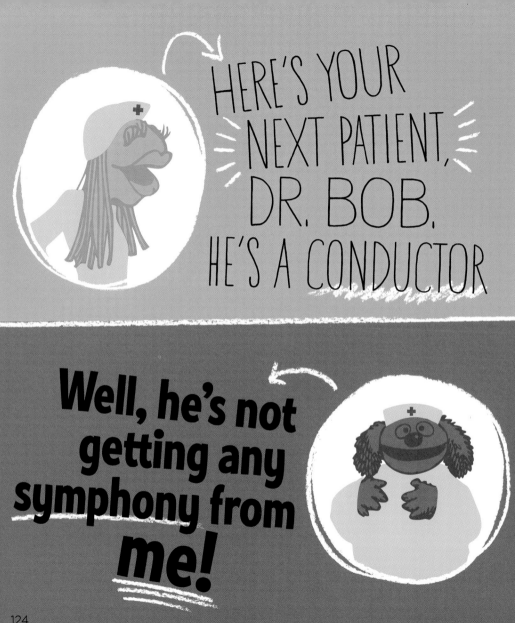

YOU MEAN SYMPATHY?

He's not getting any of that, either! ☺

WE HAVE MUSIC, COMEDY, AND 225 DANCING **ELEPHANTS** ...

WHO LEFT THEIR COSTUMES AT HOME BECAUSE UNFORTUNATELY THEY FORGOT TO PACK THEIR **TRUNKS.**

127

THEY SAY THE CHILDREN
OF TODAY ARE THE
PARENTS OF TOMORROW.

I thought it took LONGER than that..... ☺

WHAT DO YOU DO WHEN SOMEONE GIVES YOU

A LARGE BOULDER AS A PRESENT?

TAKE IT FOR GRANITE!

WOCKA!
WOCKA!

HA
HA HA HA HA HAH
HA HA HA HA

I ONCE MET A VAMPIRE SO RICH,

he lived in a split-level coffin! ☺

HOW ABOUT
THAT AUDIENCE
I PAID OFF
FOR YOU?

**What did you
tell them?**

TO GO
HOG
WILD!

I am paying you to
give me help, not cheap jokes. ☺

DR. BOB,
DO YOU THINK THE
TELEPHONE NEEDS
ANESTHETIC?

IF SO
MAKE IT A
LOCAL.

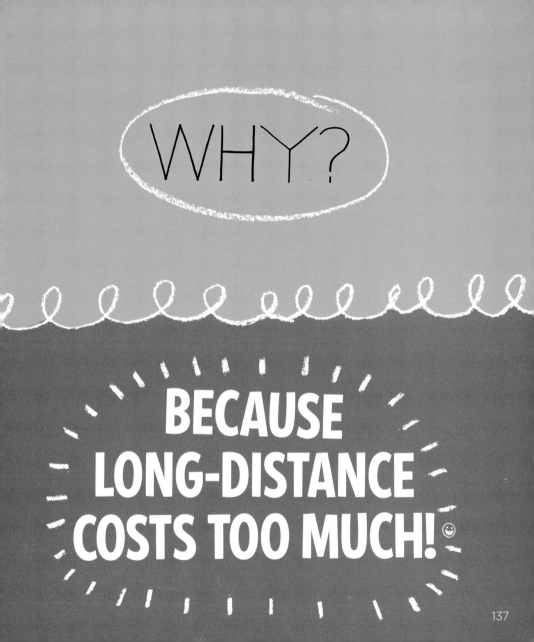

MY COUSIN IS ≋ **SO DUMB** ≋ HE THINKS EGGS BENEDICT IS A **MAFIA GANGSTER!** ☺

Kermit, what's with all those showgirls?

WE JUST KIND OF THREW THEM IN.

Well, THROW THEM OUT! ☺

THAT MAN IS ANNOYING ME.

BUT HE ISN'T EVEN LOOKING AT YOU.

That's what's ANNOYING ME! ☺

AT TIMES LIKE THIS,
I'M PROUD TO BE AN
AMERICAN! ☺

IF YOU DON'T MIND,
I'LL DO THE JOKES.

We don't mind, but
**WHEN ARE YOU
GOING TO
DO THEM?** ☺

146

YOU WANNA COME OVER TO MY HOUSE AND LISTEN TO **THE BEETLES?**

OH, I LOVE THEIR **MUSIC!**

What music? I mean REAL BEETLES... AND SOME TERMITES.... ☺

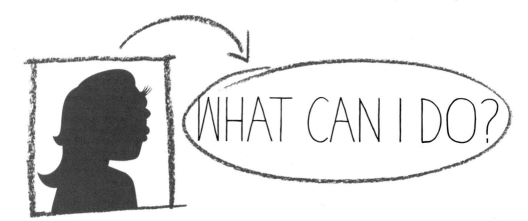

AAAH. You know, I'm falling for you.

WHAT CAN I DO?

150

Get out of the WAY!

AAAAH! ☺

Incanto il amore
my bambino!

IS THAT
ITALIAN?

No, it's
pig latin. ☺

153

WHAT KIND OF
DOG IS HE,
DR. BOB?

Ask him what time it is.

WHY?

He might be a watch dog! ☺

DR. BOB, I THINK THE
PATIENT IS RUNNING A FEVER.

Oh, well, go get **some mustard!**

HAVE YOU EVER
THOUGHT THERE MUST BE
LIFE AFTER DEATH?

Every time I leave this theater. ☺

I'M YOUR
NEW **GOPHER.**

WE HAVE FROGS AND PIGS
AND CHICKENS AROUND HERE,
BUT WE'VE
NEVER HAD
A GOPHER.

163

BØRK! BØRK! BØRK!

DE CHICKEE IN DEE BASKEE.
OOTER HEER, DEE CHICKEE,
UN OOTER DERE, DEE BASKEE.

WHAT HAS A THOUSAND LEGS BUT CAN'T WALK?

Five hundred pairs of pants! ☺

Here is a
**MUPPET
NEWS FLASH!**

DATELINE:
*The
Muppet Show.*

AN EMBARRASSING
SITUATION DEVELOPED TODAY
WHEN THE <u>MUPPET NEWS REPORTER</u>
ACCIDENTALLY WENT ON-CAMERA

**forgetting to
put on his pants. . . .**

Oh, good grief!

I KNOW WHAT'S WRONG WITH THIS SHOW. **It's the theater!**

WHAT'S WRONG WITH IT?

The seats face the stage! ☺

I HAVE A VERY POOR TRACK RECORD. ☺

Maybe he dropped it someplace.

(CONT.)

WELL, I CAN'T
DO ANYTHING ABOUT
HIS HEARING NOW.
CALL ME TOMORROW.

NO, DR. BOB,
YOU'RE RESPONSIBLE
FOR HIS EARS!

YOU'RE RIGHT! CALL ME EAR-RESPONSIBLE! ☺

WE WERE SO POOR THAT
I WAS BORN AT HOME.

After my mother saw me,
we went to the hospital. ☺

FROGS ARE **HANDSOME, DEBONAIR, & CHARMING...** WHILE TOADS ARE **UGLY AND GIVE YOU WARTS.** ☺

Dr. Bob, where did you get this patient from?

SHE WAS FOUND WITH A BUNCH OF COWS.

Not bunch, herd.

HEARD OF WHAT?

Cows.

(CONT.)

SURE, I'VE HEARD OF COWS!

No, I mean the cow's herd.

YEAH, BUT IT'S OKAY.
THE NEXT ACT WILL TAKE CARE OF IT.
Dancing Sponges, you're on! ☺

ALL'S WELL THAT ENDS WELL.

Doesn't matter to me, as long as it ends! ☺

Make me an offer. ☺

Index

Muppetational Book Fact:

How many jokes does each Muppet make?

STATLER: 15	**ROWLF:** 14	**DR. BUNSEN:** 5	**MILDRED HUXTETTER:** 3
WALDORF: 13	**CHICKEN:** 3	**MISS PIGGY:** 25	**GEORGE THE JANITOR:** 3
FOZZIE: 35	**SCOOTER:** 4	**LINK HOGTHROB:** 1	
KERMIT: 25	**GONZO:** 10	**JANICE:** 11	

HA HA HA HA HA

(CONT.)

SAM THE EAGLE: 5
ZOOT: 4
ANIMAL: 4
FLOYD PEPPER: 4

LEW ZEALAND: 1
BEAKER: 2
WHATNOT LADIES: 3
RIZZO: 2

DR. TEETH: 1
SWEDISH CHEF: 1
NEWSMAN: 1

Index (CONT.)

HA HA HA